Bryony Fairview: Weather Witch

by Rebecca Burke

Illustrated by Chris Burke

REBECCA BURKE – Author

Though Rebecca's background is more science based, having studied Sports Therapy and worked with the young physically disabled, she has always had a very big imagination and love for faery folklore and nature. When Rebecca relocated to Ireland nearly nine years ago she was able to let her imagination run wild and when her two daughters were born they became her inspiration for writing children's books.

Rebecca started writing *Bryony Fairview: Weather Witch* when climate change became a prominent feature of the news. She feels it is important for children to know and understand about the world and climate change and it is equally important to make them feel empowered and heard – knowing they have the ability to change the world. Positive language – positive thoughts!

CHRIS BURKE – Illustrator

After a lifetime of service, initially in the Defence Forces and then in the Civil Service, Chris discovered his creative side in retirement. He had had his artwork displayed in several exhibitions before being approached about *Bryony Fairview: Weather Witch*. As a Grandfather of six, he jumped at the chance to illustrate his first children's book. He has thoroughly enjoyed channelling the magic of his grandchildren into these illustrations.

First published in 2020 by Child's Eye,
Redshank Books

ISBN 978-1-912969-13-5

A CIP catalogue record for this book is
available from The British Library

Cover and design by Carnegie Book Production

Printed in the UK by Halstan

Redshank Books
Brunel House
Volunteer Way
Faringdon
Oxfordshire
SN7 7YR

Tel: +44 (0)845 873 3837

www.libripublishing.co.uk

Dedication

For my daughters Ava and Sadhbh

Chapter 1

The Beginning

Ellie looked out of the kitchen window. She was sad watching the rain; it had fallen for days and days now even though it was supposed to be summer.

It was the school holidays. Most of her friends had gone away with their families. Ellie never went away but she didn't usually mind. She lived in a small house with a wood nearby and her garden was huge and largely overgrown. Usually, she had plenty to do – looking after the garden, helping the flowers grow and listening to her mother's stories about magical fairy folk that supposedly lived there. She liked reading and had loads of books about wild plants and animals. She loved painting and drawing and making things. Ellie had a very curious mind.

Recently, she had felt restless. She didn't know why. The last time she was in the garden helping her Mum she thought she'd heard something in the bushes – a rustling,

a grumbling and then a knocking — as if something was banging against the branches. Her mother had heard too, she was sure, because she had stopped digging and had looked towards the oak tree down at the end of the garden.

'What was that?' Ellie had asked. Her Mum had smiled, 'I think we may have a visitor,' she said. That was the last time the sun had shone, and Ellie was fed up.

'Mum, I'm bored,' she moaned, 'why does it always rain here?' Her mother looked out of the window and then up to the sky, 'The Weather Witch must be sad....' she said.

Ellie's Mum loved nature; on their walks in the woods she knew all the trees and told stories about the creatures who lived among them and about the spirit folk. Sometimes, Ellie felt her mother would have loved to live right in the middle of the woods, underneath the trees.

'The Weather Witch?!' Ellie looked at her mum who now had her head tilted as if listening for something. Was her mum making up a story? For some reason Ellie didn't think so.

All sorts of thoughts flowed through her head; what was a Weather Witch? What did they look like? Where did they live? Why was she sad?

'Yes,' her mum continued 'She sometimes visits our garden, I think she likes the blueberries — there are always a lot less once she's been!'

'Have you seen her?' Ellie asked

'No, not *seen* her,' her mother replied, 'but I've heard her giggling — once, when the sun was high and the breeze light.'

Ellie could not contain her excitement — a Weather Witch in *her* garden! Who likes blueberries!! 'Right,' she thought, 'I'll go find her, cheer her up and then maybe it will be sunny again.'

This was just what Ellie needed to lift her spirits — an adventure.

Ellie grabbed a bag and filled it with important adventure essentials; nature book, binoculars, bottle of water, pencil and notebook, biscuits (lots of biscuits) and last, but possibly most important, was a tub of blueberries for the new friend she was going to find! On went her raincoat and wellies and off she went to explore the garden and find the Weather Witch....

Chapter 2

Adventure Awaits

Ellie's garden was big and very overgrown; this was going to be hard. She decided to aim for the blueberry bush first so off she went up the garden splashing in puddles as she went. She loved making big splashes in the muddy water! As she did a particularly large and impressive splash, she spotted something glistening in the flower bed ahead. Ellie ran and picked it up to investigate. To her surprise it was a beautiful, shiny, purple stone with a hole right through it; she had never seen one like it before. Ellie popped it into her pocket to keep it safe and carried on splashing up the garden.

When she got to the blueberry bush, she noticed a spider had made a large web between the leaves. She admired how beautiful the raindrops looked as they rested on the web — like precious gems on a silk thread. Then she spotted the spider; she got out her nature book to look up what type it was... 'Hmm a money spider....' Ellie concentrated, reading slowly and carefully. Her book was full of fun facts on all sorts of things.... As she continued to read, she became aware of a strange, muffled sobbing sound.

Ellie's heart raced. She hadn't really expected to find anyone in her garden despite what her mum had said.

Ellie followed the sound to the very bottom of the garden and there, facing the old oak tree, was a girl. She was wearing a long, blue cloak and on her head, she wore a pointy black hat and on the very tip of it there was, what looked like, a small thunder cloud. Very peculiar.

Ellie stepped a little closer — the girl hadn't noticed she was there; she was too busy kicking the ground, muttering, occasionally sniffing and trying to stop herself from crying.

Ellie coughed. The girl didn't notice. Ellie said, 'Excuse me, are you ok?' Without turning around, the girl replied, 'I can't talk to you.' 'Why?' asked Ellie. 'I have to think about what I've done,' the girl replied bluntly. 'Oh.' Ellie stood there for a while and then asked, 'What did you do?'

The girl turned to face Ellie and wiped a few stray tears with her sleeve. 'I rained on my sister — but I didn't mean to. She got in the way... and anyway, the flowers needed some rain.'

Rained on her sister — whatever did she mean?

The girl saw Ellie's confused look and continued 'You've never met a Weather Witch before have you?'

The Weather Witch! Ellie couldn't quite believe it – she had found the Weather Witch!

Suddenly Ellie felt embarrassed and didn't know what to say. The Weather Witch stood and stared at her curiously. 'Did you apologise?' Ellie asked shyly, 'I always find that apologising helps if I've done something I shouldn't have.'

'Yes, of course I did,' the Weather Witch said sharply, '*then* my sister noticed she'd lost her weather stone and that was apparently *my* fault too as *I'd* made her drop it when I made it rain on her...' The Weather Witch looked down at the ground and began muttering grumpily again under her breath. The thunder cloud on the tip of her hat grumbled.

'Well,' Ellie said confidently, 'We will have to find your sister's weather stone and then you can bring it back to her.'

'We?' The Weather Witch said raising her head, 'Me and you?' She looked surprised and a little confused – no one had offered to *help her* before.

'Of course! Now what does it look like?'

Just then the Weather Witch's stomach grumbled, loudly, 'Can we have a snack before we look?' she asked, 'it's hungry work thinking about what you've done, and it's been hours since breakfast!'

Ellie thought this was a good idea — she was feeling hungry too. She opened her bag and got out the tub of blueberries, offering them to her new friend, who happily and hungrily took two big handfuls. As they ate, the rain seemed to get a little lighter and the sun seemed to be trying to break through the clouds.

'Do you control the weather then, being a Weather Witch and all?' Ellie asked

'Not exactly, no,' The Weather Witch replied, 'but we do *help* control it. It's complicated. There are lots of factors involved. We help the rain to rain and the snow to fall, the sun to shine, the frost to freeze, the hailstones to hail, the rainbows to appear and when I'm old enough, I'll make thunder and lightning! Oh, I can't wait to get to make my first thunderstorm...' Ellie looked on wide-eyed as the Weather Witch grew more and more excited.

'We have to learn all the different spells and when to use them — you can't just use them willy-nilly — it has to be the right time.... When you complete each course, you get an engraving on your broom — look!' The Weather Witch grabbed her broom which was leaning against the oak tree and showed off her engravings proudly! They were beautiful; they sparkled even though the sun wasn't fully out. There was a sun at the top, directly underneath that was a raindrop and below the raindrop was a cloud.

'They're amazing!' gasped Ellie. Then she noticed a fourth engraving, not quite as neat as the others and at a slight angle 'B.F.,' she read. 'What does B F stand for?' Ellie asked.

'That's my name,' The Weather Witch said 'Bryony Fairview! Nice to meet you.' She reached for a handshake.

'She's in a better mood now she's eaten,' Ellie mused to herself as she shook Bryony's hand.

'Nice to meet you too, I'm Ellie.'

Chapter 3

The Search for the Weather Stone

Bryony jumped up, 'Let me show you what I can do!' she said excitedly and before Ellie could say anything Bryony had jumped on her broomstick and shot up into the air. Ellie could see Bryony holding up something she had taken from her pocket and heard her chant the words 'solas na gréine,' three times.

'Now watch the nimbostratus!' Bryony shouted and pointed towards the grey clouds overhead. Ellie looked up to the clouds and as she did, she saw them separate and saw the sun shine through. She couldn't believe her eyes. Bryony flew back down to Ellie, looking very proud of herself. 'Easy!' She said with a grin.

'Wow,' Ellie gasped, 'that was amazing! How did you make the sun break through so easily? Were they magical words? Just wow!'

Bryony smiled, 'That was the spell — the words meant sunshine. I spoke them to ask the sun to shine brighter and, by using my weather stone, and a little bit of magic, my words were carried to the sun.'

Suddenly the girls remembered. They looked at each other 'Oh! The weather stone!' they said.

Bryony pulled her stone out of her pocket and showed it to Ellie 'This is what a weather stone is, though my sister's is purple.'

Bryony had a shimmering blue pebble with a hole right through it in her hand. Ellie instantly recognised the stone. 'Look! I've already found it!' she said excitedly, fumbling about in her pocket, but all her hand found was a big hole. 'Oh,' Ellie said sadly, 'it must have fallen out.'

'It could be anywhere now!' Bryony sighed, looking round at the big garden.

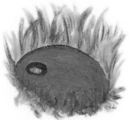

Ellie thought for a while. All they needed was a plan. Ellie was good at making plans. 'That's it!' she thought. 'All we need to do is re-trace my footsteps!' Ellie said, as she rummaged in her backpack. 'And we can use these too!' She pulled out her binoculars triumphantly – a holey pocket was not going to stop them re- finding the weather stone!

The two new friends set off down the garden, each taking turns looking through the binoculars, chatting and jumping in the odd puddle here and there. (Bryony liked puddles too.)

'I'm learning how to make rainbows appear next,' Bryony explained, 'my sister is excellent at making them. It's quite hard – you must make sure the rain falls just 'so' for the sun to shine through in a particular way so making the right colours in the right order. Once I've learnt how to control all the different types of weathers I will then go to my final station to perfect my chosen weather element, like all the young Weather Witches do. What do you do at school?' Bryony asked as Ellie passed her the binoculars.

'Maths, English and Science mainly, sometimes we do PE. I do like school, but it can be a bit boring. Nothing like flying in the sky and making the weather change,' Ellie said enviously. 'Though we do go on school trips sometimes, they're always fun.'

'Wahoo!' Bryony suddenly squealed.

'Did you find it?' Ellie asked.

'No, but I found the blueberry bush and there are some blueberries just ripe for the picking! Yum!' Bryony put down the binoculars and started to pick the blueberries. Ellie sighed, 'Mmmm, must be hungry work being a Weather Witch,' she thought, 'I'm still full from the last lot of blueberries!'

Ellie leant down to pick up the binoculars and as she did so, she saw a little purple glimmer in the soil by the bush. Yes! There it was — the weather stone, shimmering beautifully in the sunlight.

'I found it!' she shouted, holding it up to show Bryony, who was just putting the last blueberry in her mouth. Bryony clapped her hands together happily. 'Thank you Ellie! Thank you, my sister will be so pleased!' Bryony grinned from ear to ear as she put the weather stone safely in her pocket. Ellie blushed. 'We should celebrate,' Bryony continued, 'Do you have anything else in your backpack?'

'Just some water and these...,' Ellie answered pulling out the biscuits, having guessed Bryony would like one — or two.

'They're perfect for celebrating!' Bryony said reaching out and taking a couple of biscuits, then one more which she put in her pocket. 'Thank you and thank you again,' she said. Ellie smiled. She'd had a fun day and had made a new, and very hungry, friend. Bryony smiled back.

'Ellie! Your dinner's ready!' The familiar voice reached Ellie from the house. 'Is that your Mum?' asked Bryony.

'Mmm, I'd better go,' Ellie said sadly.

Bryony looked up at the sky, 'Me too, it's nearly evening. I don't want to be out then!'

'Why? Are there night-time Weather Witches too?' Ellie asked a little nervously.

'Yes, we call them the elders, they're horrible and tonight they're having a big meeting so there will be loads of them!' Bryony said. 'They always want to squeeze your cheeks and insist on giving you boiled sweets! Yuck!' Bryony started to get on her broomstick. 'I've had a really lovely day with you today, Ellie, thank you friend.'

'Me too,' Ellie agreed, 'Will I ever see you again?'

'Definitely! And bring biscuits!' Bryony smiled then off she flew waving happily down at Ellie. Ellie waved back and watched as Bryony flew up and up, until she was out of sight. Then she packed up her bag and made her way in for dinner.

Chapter 4

The Land behind the Clouds

That night there was a terrible storm. Ellie thought about the meeting of the elder Weather Witches Bryony had mentioned and couldn't help but feel scared. She wished she'd asked Bryony why they were meeting. She wished she understood more, but all she could do was listen to the howling winds and the rain beating against her bedroom window.

The following day though, the sun was shining, and Ellie searched the sky to see if she could see her friend. She wondered what Bryony was doing and how she was getting on with her rainbow-making class. She wondered if Bryony's sister had been pleased with the return of her stone and if Bryony had told her sister about her, Ellie.

As she looked, she saw a beautiful rainbow appear as if by magic over her garden. There was no rain or clouds. 'It must be Bryony,' she thought. Ellie smiled. Yesterday had been so exciting — she couldn't wait for their next adventure together.

As Ellie admired the rainbow, she saw something, or someone, flying to the ground; she quickly put on her shoes and ran out to her garden. She went to the old oak tree where she and Bryony had first met and there Bryony stood again, out of breath and looking rather worried.

'Is everything ok?' Ellie asked

'Oh dear, dear. I don't know what to do, but we must do something. Oh dear, dear,' Bryony paced around the oak tree.

'What's wrong? What's happened?' Ellie asked again

'The elders are angry — storms are coming — our magic is not enough — the earth is angry. Panic everywhere.' Bryony, ignoring her friend's questioning, stumbled over her words in a panic. She suddenly stopped and looked up at Ellie, with a little hope in her eyes. 'You have to come with me,' she said.

'Come where?' Ellie was worried but still not really sure as to why.

'To my land behind the clouds. Don't worry, I'll keep you safe, I just know if the elder Mayweather sisters meet you, they will be less angry, they'll see your kind aren't all bad.' Ellie could see Bryony was forming a plan. She did trust her friend and wanted to help. She feared the storms that Bryony said were coming, but she wasn't sure how her meeting the elder Mayweather sisters would help.

'Ok,' Ellie finally agreed. 'But I must let my mum know I'm going somewhere, wait here.' And with that she started to run back to her house

'Bring biscuits!' Bryony called.

After a while Ellie returned — with her bag in tow. 'Don't worry I have made sure to bring a *whole* pack of biscuits,' she reassured Bryony as she walked up to her. Bryony mounted her broom and motioned for Ellie to climb on the back. Ellie nervously climbed aboard and held on tightly.

'Oh,' Bryony remembered and passed back a pair of goggles to Ellie, 'put these on — they will protect your eyes as we pass through to the land behind the clouds.' Ellie put them on and then quickly grabbed hold of the broom again. Off they went — higher and higher — so high Ellie could hardly breathe! She clung on to the broom, closed her eyes and tried to catch a breath.

Suddenly the broom felt as if it had stopped and Ellie found she could breathe normally again. She slowly opened her eyes. They were still moving through the air but were definitely not above her garden anymore. The land below her was not the same as her own but not completely unknown to her either. She'd seen pictures of it she was sure, but where? Before she could remember Bryony called 'Are you ok? I'm going to land soon, let me know if you feel a little queasy, I can get you some hot cocoa, that'll help, then we'll head straight over to the Mayweather sisters.' Ellie couldn't muster up any words so only nodded in reply.

Bryony started the descent, it felt very smooth, almost like they were barely moving at all. Ellie looked down to see beautifully coloured buildings all with different types of roofs. There was one in particular that Ellie seemed drawn to. It was a little smaller than the others, was an emerald green colour and had a roof of higgledy piggledy slates rising up to a point. At the very top there was a golden weathervane with N/E/S/W marked on it. As they got lower Ellie could no longer see the green house. They had almost reached the cobbled street below, but these were no ordinary cobbles, they glimmered and shone and were all different colours — pinks, blues, oranges, greens — every colour you could imagine.

The landing was as smooth as the descent had been. Bryony jumped off and helped Ellie to climb off. Ellie's legs felt unsteady and Bryony held her arm. 'Don't worry, I was a little wobbly after my first flight too, you get used to it. Come on let's get some cocoa — you look like you need one. I wouldn't say no myself either!'

Bryony led Ellie down the street and into a little pink building. The sign above the door read Ciara's Café. 'Brooms down the best cocoa you'll get in the land here!' Bryony smiled as she ushered Ellie into a little seat in a corner.

The café was busy. Bryony vanished for a few minutes and when she returned, she was holding two enormous goblets in her hands. Steam shimmered up from the goblets, sparkling as if it was full of tiny stars. Bryony blew away the steam from her cocoa and took a big sip. Ellie did the same. Almost at once she felt less wobbly and the warmth of the cocoa comforted her and made her feel a little calmer. Ellie took another bigger sip.

'Mmmm,' she murmured. 'Good, eh?' Bryony said with a grin.

Once they had finished their cocoas, Bryony decided it was best to walk to the Mayweather Sisters' house as it was not far, and she could explain things to Ellie as best she could on the way.

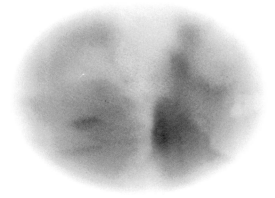

Chapter 5

The Mayweather Sisters

Ellie gazed around her as they strolled. The cobbles sparkled like gemstones and the houses were just as beautiful – pinks, blues, greens, purples – there was so much colour everywhere in Bryony's world!

Bryony explained to Ellie that the Mayweather sisters were the oldest Weather Witches in the area and were twins, although they looked nothing like each other, nor acted alike. She explained that they were the ones who had called the meeting of all the elders, but it had not gone to plan. The storms were

so wild the night before, she said because the meeting had turned into an argument causing the elders from each corner of the Weather Witch world to clash.

'The weather is becoming harder to control,' explained Bryony, 'and our magic seems to be becoming weaker. I'm not sure why, but I have heard whispers that the earth is angry and if we don't resolve it, we may all vanish in the storms — just like the Earth Witches vanished many moons ago.' They turned a corner down a narrow alleyway. At the bottom of the alley was a tall, narrow, purple building with golden windowpanes and a large golden door.

Ellie had so many questions she wanted to ask but it was clear they had arrived at their destination and Bryony seemed eager to go inside.

'Bryony,' Ellie said, 'what exactly is your plan?' Bryony knocked on the big golden door and turned to Ellie. 'I haven't got one yet, but I'm sure it will come to me.' Ellie's heart sank as the door opened.

A young woman stood in the doorway and motioned for the girls to come inside.

'The sisters are in the study,' she whispered, 'I'm sure they won't mind if you pop up but be sure to knock.' She gave Bryony a little nudge and Ellie a hard stare before scurrying off down the hall.

'Come on,' Bryony said confidently as she started up the winding stairs. Ellie followed her up and up the seemingly never-ending staircase.

'Any plan yet?' Ellie asked. 'Not just yet but I can feel it in my bones one is coming,' Bryony said a little out of breath. Then as they neared the top Bryony suddenly stopped and turned to Ellie. 'Maeve is the nice one, she'll be sure to help. Elodie... well, don't look at Elodie. She has a temper and doesn't really like your kind. But I'm sure she'll be fine.' and with that Bryony turned and knocked on a small wooden door.

Ellie wished Bryony would stop telling her things like this just before knocking on doors — she really wasn't giving her any time to process things.

'Come in!' Two voices called simultaneously from behind the door. Bryony sensed Ellie's upset. 'I promise you it will be ok,' she reassured her with a whisper, 'we will work this out together. Thank you for coming here with me, my friend.' Bryony took Ellie's hand and opened the door. Ellie felt a little better and followed her friend through the small wooden door.

 Inside the room they found two old women looking down at a large map which was opened out flat on a table. The Mayweather sisters were taller than Ellie had expected. They both wore trousers and their hat points were folded over

and tucked into the rim at the back of the hat. One wore thic-rimmed glasses and her hair was full of wild curls, the other had short hair. They barely looked at Bryony and Ellie as the two entered the cluttered room.

'Come in, come in,' the first sister said, 'Now Bryony, who have you got here?' and, with a sly little smile and a nod to Bryony, she continued, 'have you been exploring the other land again?' Ellie liked her.

The room itself was dark and had lots and lots of books and what looked like aviation memorabilia. There were black and white photos of the sisters up on the wall, though from when they were much, much, younger.

'This is Ellie, Ellie this is Maeve Mayweather.' The curly-haired sister smiled and waved to Ellie. 'And that,' continued Bryony, 'is Elodie Mayweather.' She pointed over to the short-haired sister and immediately dropped her arm as Elodie turned to look.

'Nice to meet you both,' Ellie said shyly.

Elodie did not look happy to see either Bryony or Ellie. Ellie glanced down to the map the sisters had been studying and saw it wasn't like any map she'd ever seen before. There were clouds instead of land and symbols showing different types

of weather and it almost looked as though the clouds were moving and swirling. Elodie quickly rolled up the map as she saw Ellie looking at it. 'Why have you brought her here?' Elodie asked Bryony sharply.

'Err, well, Ellie helped me yesterday with something very important and was very kind and I heard the earth was angry and I thought as our magic grows weaker if the humankind show more kindness to the earth maybe, just maybe, it will be less angry.' Bryony replied. Elodie snorted in disgust as she packed the rolled-up map in a carry case.

'Sister, be kind,' Maeve said as she placed her hand on Elodie's. 'Bryony is trying to help, and she does make a nice point.'

Elodie shrugged Maeve's hand away. 'Humankind starts being kind? Oh, then, suddenly, everything is right as rain? Please! Stronger magic is what is needed, what magic does humankind have?'

'But sister, some people say humankind are descendants of Earth Witches,' Maeve said calmly.

'Some people are wrong,' Elodie replied bluntly.

'Sister you forget...' but before Maeve could continue, Elodie began in a sharper and louder voice — 'No sister, it is you who forgets. You forget what humankind is capable of. The Earth

Witches were no match for them and now there are none left. And what can a human *child* do to help us when her elders know no better than destruction and waste?'

'We must teach them,' said Maeve. 'They are not all the same; you out of everyone should know that!'

'I know they are of no help here and should never be in our world.' Elodie glared at Ellie and stormed out of the room and slammed the door, knocking a picture off the wall. Ellie immediately retrieved the picture and glanced at it while handing it to Maeve.

'Forgive my sister, girls. She has not always been so bitter. There was a time she spent many a moon in your world.' She smiled and wiped some dust from the frame as she hung it back up. The photograph showed a young Elodie holding her broom, proudly showing off her final engravings, smiling from ear to ear.

'It's been a while since I've seen that smile.' Maeve seemed lost in thought for a moment. 'Now Bryony,' said Maeve, returning to the present, 'what is your plan? You surely knew this would not go smoothly. How are you children going to rescue our worlds?'

Bryony and Ellie looked at each other, then to the floor. 'I really didn't have a plan as such,' Bryony stuttered 'I just felt it was the right thing to do. Ellie helped me yesterday and was so kind and I felt if we work together, surely, we can do *something* — she brought biscuits.' Bryony motioned to Ellie to pass her the biscuits. Maeve gave a small smile; she could see Bryony meant well.

'Well, in that case let's have a sit down and a biscuit and then you must return Ellie home. She does not belong here; she is not safe here. The elders are all gathering again in three days and hopefully, it will end better this time.'

Both girls were very disappointed. Ellie wasn't ready to go home, and Bryony was not ready to give up. She knew in her bones they could help. They just needed a plan, that was all — and a good one.

The friends walked slowly back to the café in silence barely looking up from the ground. 'Three days,' thought Ellie, 'three days isn't long to save both worlds.' She almost felt like she wanted to cry. Bryony kept looking like she had something to say then stopping herself and returning to look back at the floor.

As they turned a corner, they bumped into a girl who had been

 carrying a pile of books that were now all over the street. 'BRYONY!' the girl shouted. Bryony jumped back and looked up — 'Oh it's you,' she said to the girl 'you should look where you're going.'

'You should look where you're going,' the girl replied grumpily, 'and who is this you're with, I don't recognise her.'

'That's because you don't know her. She's Ellie, MY friend.' Bryony turned to Ellie, 'Ellie, this is my sister Hazel.' Ellie could tell they were not the closest of sisters. She put out her hand for a handshake, but Hazel just looked at her.

'Well, help me pick up the books then,' she said rudely. Ellie, Bryony and Hazel began collecting the scattered books. 'Which class are you in then?' Hazel asked Ellie. 'Erm,' Ellie wasn't really sure how to answer, then ... 'she's not from this world,' Bryony butted in, almost seeming to be showing off with the remark.

Hazel's face dropped then she looked at Bryony with a smug face saying, 'Oh you are going to be in so much trouble!' and with that, Hazel grabbed the last of her books and ran off.

Bryony looked aghast and she went to call after her, but something stopped her and instead she started walking a little faster back to where she'd left her broom.

Something seemed different all of a sudden, although they had passed many Weather Witches earlier, now as they walked on Ellie noticed everyone had begun to stare at them — at her — and this made her feel quite uncomfortable. Ellie

urged Bryony to walk even faster. She started to feel very unwelcome and wanted to go home. She wanted her mum.

'I think I *had* better go home now. Mum will be wondering where I am,' she said meekly to Bryony. This made Bryony stop in her tracks 'But you will come back, won't you?' She asked in a panic. Ellie couldn't muster up any words and she was afraid she'd start to cry, so instead she just nodded even though she was unsure she would be.

Chapter 6

A Family Secret Revealed

When they arrived back at the oak tree Bryony hugged Ellie tightly and said goodbye.

Ellie waved as Bryony flew away, then she turned and ran to her house, tears streaming down her face. She ran in the front door and there was her mum — she fell into her arms and sobbed.

'Oh Ellie, what's wrong?' Her mother asked. Ellie told her mother all that had happened that day and the day before. She told her about Bryony, Hazel and the two Mayweather sisters, the weather stone, the land behind the clouds, the colourful houses, the storms, the magic becoming weaker and the stares. She started to cry harder.

Ellie's mother hugged her and kissed her head. Ellie looked up at her mother. She was expecting her to say it was a dream or 'what an imagination you have' but instead she said, 'Oh my love. There's something I must tell you.'

Ellie's mother led her up the stairs and into the attic. She moved some boxes out of the way and pulled an old suitcase towards her, blowing off some of the dust that had gathered on it.

'This is your great grandmother's suitcase; it has some of her most precious items including her diary and some letters.' She opened the case and Ellie peered inside. 'You see, Ellie,' her mother continued as she pulled out a hat from the suitcase, 'Your great grandmother was one of the last known Earth Witches.'

Ellie stared wide eyed at the hat in her mother's hands. It was pointy like Bryony's, but it was a brown colour and had an oak leaf at the tip. She felt a smile appear on her face and her mind started to race.

Ellie's mother smiled, 'Yes, we are descendants of the Earth Witches. I was first told when I was about your age and now it is time for you to learn about our family history.'

She passed Ellie the hat and reached back into the suitcase to retrieve a small, black and white photograph, similar to the ones Ellie had seen in the Mayweather sisters' study.

'Many years ago when your great grandmother was a young woman she would help to heal the earth and help the flowers and trees to grow, but there arose a dreadful fear among the Earth Witches — humankind were building faster than the witches could grow and the earth began to suffer. The Earth Witches had many, many meetings and finally decided their magic alone was not enough to help heal the earth. They decided that they themselves would become trees — trees that would forever grow and be unable to be cut down. They would help the Earth grow stronger from deep within.'

She paused and looked at the photo before continuing, 'Your grandmother was only a young girl when her mother decided to give herself to the earth. The elders grew into magnificent trees and the plan seemed to have worked for many years, but now the Earth is struggling again. I have felt it in the soil and heard it from the trees.'

Ellie stared at her mum, unable to grasp everything she had been told. 'But where are all the others? There must be more.' Her mother looked down. 'The remaining

Earth Witches were very young and were scared, they decided to live as humans. I know of no others.'

Ellie gazed at the picture; it wasn't the best quality though Ellie *could* just about make out that it was her great grandmother holding her grandmother in her arms. She was posing with another young woman. Ellie screwed up her eyes and looked harder at the picture and was sure she recognised the other woman, but could it be?

'That's Elodie Mayweather!' She suddenly said. 'I'm sure of it! They look so happy.'

'That's your great grandmother and her best friend; they were inseparable mum used to say. They had many adventures together and were always laughing. But she never saw her again after her mother changed.'

Ellie couldn't imagine Elodie laughing or being fun but then wondered if this was the reason she was so grumpy. It must have been sad losing her best friend. Then she started to think of Bryony and how sad she would be if she didn't see her again. 'Mum,' she said, 'I need to go back and help Bryony.'

'I know,' Her mother replied 'I believe in you both, you will be safe. But right now, how about something to eat?'

Ellie suddenly realised how hungry she was and, helping her mother carry the suitcase downstairs, she happily sat at the dinner table and ate.

That evening Ellie and her mother spoke about everything, Ellie asked lots of questions and her mother did her best to answer them all. There was something that kept replaying in Ellie's mind, why did the elders change into trees why not into flowers or grass?

'Trees,' her mother explained, 'trees are amazing things; not only can they be strong and beautiful — they help the earth. Some provide berries and nuts for the creatures; they provide shelter and most importantly they absorb carbon dioxide and release oxygen helping to balance the elements of planet earth.'

So, trees help the balance of elements — magic is an element — or at least that's what Ellie had heard Bryony say — maybe trees are still the answer...

Chapter 7

The Special Necklace

That night Ellie barely slept, she researched the weather patterns of recent years and the effects trees have on the environment and, slowly but surely, a plan started to come.

She studied her great grandmother's suitcase, looking at her pictures and reading her letters and diary. There was one diary entry she particularly liked. It read:

'Elodie came over today, we met at the end of the garden as usual – she was in a particularly good mood. She said she'd just learnt how to make a thunderstorm! She was so happy with herself and desperate to show off! I never say no to an adventure.... We went to the empty field behind the house and she was going to show me a bolt of lightning, followed by a roll of thunder – I made sure we were far enough away from the trees and the seedlings – I did not want all my hard work ruined! (My plan is to make the field into a forest, eventually anyway!) Elodie flew up into the air and called out her magic words holding her weather stone high. I should have known something bad was going to happen because the trees all shivered! There it was — the brightest lightning bolt I have ever seen, followed almost seconds after by the loudest clash of thunder! It was magnificent! But then we heard another sound, closer to the ground a creaking cracking then a thud.... The lightning had struck the electricity pylon beyond the field and knocked it down.... The whole village is without electricity! I wonder if it will be reported in the paper, I can just imagine the headlines 'Freak Lightning Strike on Beautiful Sunny Day' maybe something catchier though. I have never seen Elodie go so pale or fly so fast — she was so worried. She needn't be though, no one was hurt, and it won't do anyone any harm to live without electricity for a while....'

To Ellie, these little excerpts showed Elodie in a completely new light — she reminded her a bit of Bryony — but it was getting late and Ellie knew she had a big couple of days coming up. Warm and comfortable and with her great grandmother's happy thoughts running through her head she was able to drift off to a much-needed sleep.

The following morning Ellie woke feeling more confident. She got out her backpack and started to fill it with all the bits she was going to need. She made sure to pack her great grandmother's hat and the picture

of her with Elodie; she wanted to give it to Elodie and hoped it would make her at least smile a little again; and, of course, biscuits for Bryony. There was one more thing she knew was needed but she would collect that on the way up to the oak tree.

Ellie almost skipped down the stairs, she felt surer of herself today and wanted to get her plan in motion. Despite this, as she started to head to the back door, Ellie felt a wave of uncertainty come over her.

Her mother walked up to her. 'Here Ellie,' she said 'wear this,' and with that she took off her necklace, which Ellie had never seen her do before. The pendant was a small gold and silver acorn and leaf — it was beautiful.

'But that's your special necklace,' Ellie said.

'It was my mother's, and her mother's before, and now it is yours.' Ellie's mother put the necklace around Ellie's neck.

'My mother always said that it was a magic necklace and would give me the strength of all the Earth Witches at my times of need — now I feel your time of need is greater than mine. Know I will be with you too. I love you and I believe in you. You are amazing.' Ellie's mum hugged her tight and kissed her head.

'Thank you, mum, I love you too.' Ellie said as she walked out of the door, but before she closed it behind her she looked back at her mum with a smile 'I've got this,' she said.

Chapter 8

The Forbidden Book and the Weather Rock

As Ellie walked up the garden she eagerly looked for seeds, but she couldn't find any and before she knew it, she was at the oak tree where Bryony was already waiting for her. 'Are you ready?' Bryony eagerly asked. 'Not quite,' Ellie said, still searching for any sort of seed she could find. 'I just need one more thing for my plan...'

'You've got a plan! Brilliant!' said Bryony, 'I couldn't think of anything!' Ellie looked at her and frowned. 'Err, well, I had a

 *kind* of plan, but it mainly consisted of bringing you back and *you* having a plan.... So, I guess it did kind of work.' Ellie rolled her eyes.

'Come on though we really haven't got too much longer,' Bryony continued. 'Ok,' Ellie said. She felt maybe she could find a seed from Bryony's land and that would work just as well. They hopped on Bryony's broom, Ellie put on the goggles, and off they flew.

Ellie didn't feel as wobbly this time after the journey, but still felt a little nervous flying. Bryony had decided it was best to go to hers this time and properly go through the plan before going back to the Mayweather sisters.

Bryony's house was small and red. No one seemed to be at home, but Bryony still rushed Ellie upstairs just in case. Her bedroom was quite tidy, which surprised Ellie, and her bed was a hammock strung up between the walls. There was a small desk which had books and papers strewn on top – lots with doodles of thunderbolts. Bryony cleared the desk and pushed a stool towards Ellie, motioning her to sit.

Ellie sat down and opened her bag, she couldn't wait to tell Bryony what she had found out about her family the night before, but before she could say anything there was a loud bang from downstairs and the room shook.

The bang had made both girls jump and they sat in silence almost too scared to breathe. They listened and heard footsteps running up the

stairs. The footsteps continued past Bryony's door and then there was another loud bang of a door.

'Phew,' whispered Bryony 'It's only Hazel.' Ellie gave a sigh of relief. Bryony went to her door and put her ear against it. 'I wonder why she's so upset, I've never heard her slam the doors quite so loud before...' Bryony looked at Ellie with a kind of smirk. 'Shall we go listen at her bedroom door?' Ellie knew they shouldn't but was just too curious as to why she had stormed past in the way she did.

They tiptoed down the hall and quietly listened from outside Hazel's room. There were a lot of bangs and thuds coming from the other side of the door. They could hear Hazel muttering to herself: 'Where is it? There must be a spell to fix it! Oh, what have I done!' she sounded very upset.

Ellie, trying to be as quiet as she could, motioned to Bryony: should they knock on the door and help her? Bryony shook her head frantically, 'No way!' she whispered. Just then the door opened. Both girls stumbled over each other trying to get back up the hall and away from the door, but they were too late, they'd been seen.

 There in the doorway, looking like thunder was Hazel. She had obviously been crying and did not look happy to see either Bryony or Ellie.

'What are you doing?' She thundered at the friends who were now at Bryony's bedroom door. 'Nothing,' Bryony said quickly and continued, 'but what have you done though?' Hazel went pale and couldn't help but burst into tears.

'Maybe we can help?' Ellie said, feeling so bad to have made Hazel cry. Sniffing, Hazel replied, 'I don't think you can. I don't think anyone can and tomorrow the elders will be here, and they will be so angry with me.' There was so much worry in her voice that even Bryony felt bad for her — although she was also pleased to hear it was Hazel who would be getting into trouble and not her for a change.

'We can try,' Bryony said. Hazel smiled in response and disappeared in her room for a few seconds, returning with a large black book. She held it up to show the two of them; it read, 'Spells and Magic for the Curious Witch.' Bryony gasped, though something had obviously been lost on Ellie as she was not sure of the significance of this book.

'We're not supposed to read that!' Bryony said in shock, 'Did you try one of the spells? You did, didn't you!'

Bryony turned to Ellie. 'That book is forbidden for young Weather Witches! It contains some powerful spells — too powerful for us to control and can be so dangerous!' Ellie looked at Hazel who was looking very scared.

'Yes, all right Bryony, I shouldn't be reading it, but I really wanted to help. I thought I could possibly find a spell to make our magic stronger. I was practising a couple of small spells, nothing too dangerous, then it happened.' She looked down and croaked the last bit 'the Weather Rock cracked.'

Bryony's eyes widened, and her mouth gaped opened. Ellie had not heard of the Weather Rock before but it cracking did not sound good. Hazel started to cry again.

Once Hazel had stopped crying the three girls decided they should go and take a look at the Weather Rock. Maybe Hazel was mistaken, maybe the crack wasn't as big as she'd first thought.

They walked down the cobbled streets, beyond the buildings, to a large open space. There were no vivid colours here, not like the other parts of this land, instead it was just muted greys and whites. At the very back of this eerie space was a large rock. This, the sisters explained to Ellie, was the Weather Rock. Each time a Weather Witch was born it released a weather stone which would then belong to that Weather Witch for life.

 'It has been many years since it's produced any weather stones. Bryony and I are some of the youngest Weather Witches here,' Hazel explained to Ellie as they walked up to it. 'It

once shone with beautiful colours, but now it is grey like the rest of this area.'

Bryony walked around the rock examining it for the crack Hazel said she had made in it. She suddenly stopped in her tracks. 'Hazel,' she gasped, 'it's an enormous crack! It's nearly broken in two!!' Hazel went white and both she and Ellie ran around to where Bryony stood. There, running almost the complete height of the rock was the crack.

'I'm not sure we'll be able to hide this,' Ellie sadly said.

'They'll definitely notice it!' Bryony continued.

Hazel put her head in her hands. 'What am I going to do?'

Before they could come up with any ideas there was a loud siren. The girls looked at each other.

'That's the safety call, how odd. We must go home straight away!' Hazel turned and hurried Ellie and Bryony back to the cobbled streets and home.

Chapter 9

Baking Up a Plan

The girls passed lots of other Weather Witches on the way back. No one seemed to notice Ellie. There was panic in the air. Bryony and Hazel's mother was at the house when they arrived. She was sat in the kitchen and she called Bryony through to her. Ellie crept up the stairs and back to Bryony's room, managing not to be seen by their mother.

'Hazel,' their mother said 'Please watch Bryony and please *try* to both get on. The elders are arriving tonight...'

'But they're not supposed to arrive until tomorrow, why are they coming today?' Hazel asked with great concern.

'They feel the Mayweathers have had long enough to come

 up with a plan and have lost their patience. They have said they must now take matters into their own hands.'

'That does not sound good,' Bryony said, subconsciously glancing towards the stairs. Her mother glared at her.

'You have not brought back that human girl again? Did you not get into enough trouble yesterday?' Bryony looked down at the ground. 'She is not safe here; you must hide her in this house until the elders have gone. Do not let anyone in and do not leave this house until I am back and have made sure it is safe enough for you to take her home. Honestly Bryony I do not know what I am going to do with you.' With that their mother grabbed her broom, hat and cloak and left, slamming the door behind her. Bryony and Hazel stood and looked at each other for a while before heading up to find Ellie.

As they walked into Bryony's room, they saw Ellie had emptied her backpack and was wearing an Earth Witch's hat on her head. Bryony ran to Ellie, 'I've never seen a real Earth Witch's hat before,' she said excitedly 'is it yours?'

Hazel grunted 'Of course it's not! It's not a real one.'

'It is!' Ellie argued, 'Well, it's my great grandmother's. But it's still technically mine. My great grandmother was an Earth Witch and I am a direct descendant from her.' Ellie finished confidently and held her head high.

Hazel slowly walked towards her, examining the hat. 'Hmmm. Maybe it does look real,' she eventually concluded.

Without looking up at Hazel, Bryony scoffed 'Like you would know, you've never seen one before either!' Still looking at the hat in awe, she continued, 'So...how *did* you get it?'

'I told you,' said Ellie proudly, with her head held high. 'It was my great grandmother's.'

It took a little while for Ellie's announcement to sink in. Seeing the two sisters looking completely baffled Ellie told them everything her mother had said the night before. They listened, amazed and although Hazel didn't seem entirely convinced, Bryony was delighted. 'I knew it!' she clapped her hands 'I knew it! I knew it! I knew it!'

She looked at Ellie with a broad smile. 'So what's the plan my Earth sister?' Ellie smiled and started to tell them her plan. Bryony listened intently; Hazel listened, but it was clear by her face that she was not convinced it would work.

'... so you see' concluded Ellie, 'I still need one more thing for

the plan to work. A seed. I couldn't find any in my garden so we must find one here and then head to the meeting of the elders.' Bryony and

Hazel's faces dropped and they looked at each other and then at Ellie.

'You can't leave the house, neither of you can,' Hazel said bluntly.

'But, but, we must!' Ellie pleaded. Hazel crossed her arms sternly and shook her head. Bryony put her hand on Ellie's arm signalling her that this was ok.

'No, Ellie,' she said, 'Hazel is right, we can't leave the house – it's too dangerous.' Bryony stood up and continued 'I fancy baking...'

'You can't bake, you can't even make toast properly!' Hazel sneered.

'Well, as we may be stuck here for some time I'll have time to learn,' Bryony said and with that she headed downstairs to the kitchen. Ellie followed quickly behind. Hazel tutted and headed into her room, there was no way she was going to be dragged into trying Bryony's creations or cleaning up after her!

'Is that it?' Ellie asked Bryony as she watched her get down a mixing bowl and rummage in cupboards for ingredients. 'Are we giving up and baking biscuits for the night?'

'Oh no, we're not baking biscuits,' Bryony said and started to hum a little tune as she went from one cupboard to the next. By this point Ellie was utterly confused. What was Bryony up to? Then Bryony turned to look at Ellie while holding a big tub of something. 'We're making...' she paused and looked around making sure Hazel wasn't there and with a whisper said, 'we're making glue'

Ellie smiled as she started to understand Bryony's sudden need for baking. 'I'm awful at baking edible things but stodgy, stick your jaws together, gloopy stuff I am the expert in! Hazel won't come out of her room for fear of either being made to sample the baking or tidying up the mess we may make. She'll have her door shut as usual and so we can use the batter to stick her door fast shut then all we need to do is walk out of the front door.' Bryony was beaming as she relayed her plan to Ellie.

It didn't take more than five minutes to get the batter nice and sticky, the girls then crept upstairs and smothered the batter all over Hazel's door. They ran as quietly as they could down the stairs and to the front door, leaving the remaining batter in the bowl by Hazel's door, then out to the streets they went.

The streets were empty, there was a strange atmosphere — quite unsettling — but the girls knew they needed to act fast to get Ellie's plan in motion.

Bryony grabbed her broomstick and looking up at the sky turned to Ellie. 'I don't think we have time to find a seed, the other elders are close, the meeting is about to begin and we must get there in time to hide before they arrive.' Ellie glanced down at her mother's necklace and held the acorn in her hand 'I think I may already have the exact seed I need,' she replied to Bryony.

Bryony jumped on her broom. 'We'll be too heavy to go at the speed we need if we both travel on my broom. How do you feel about cloud travel?'

Before Ellie could figure out what cloud travel was and how she felt about it Bryony had her weather stone in her hand and it was glowing blue — 'scamaill agus gaoth,' she said three times. Suddenly a cloud appeared under Ellie lifting her up in the air.

'The cloud won't last long but should last enough time to get us there. Quickly now follow me.' Ellie had no idea how she was going to follow Bryony as she had never flown on a cloud before, but to her relief the cloud seemed to know what to do and followed Bryony's broom automatically.

As they arrived at the colourless space where the now grey and cracked Weather Rock stood, the cloud descended to just above the ground and dissipated. Ellie fell to the ground with a thud.

'Sorry,' Bryony said 'I should have warned you about that happening.' Ellie got up and dusted herself off. The skies began to grow dark and cold — very, very, cold. Bryony pulled Ellie behind the Weather Rock and crouched down. The rock was large enough to hide both girls sufficiently, though they both wished they were invisible as the realisation of many angry elders arriving soon dawned on them both and terrified them.

The atmosphere grew colder and colder and flurries of snow started to fall all around them. 'Snow,' Bryony whispered to Ellie, 'the Weather Witches from the North are arriving.' Ellie looked to the sky and saw five Weather Witches all in greys and whites swirling down on their brooms.

Before the five witches had even landed, the skies changed and rain started to fall harder and harder. Covering her head with her cloak Bryony whispered again to Ellie, 'These are the Weather Witches from the East.' Ellie could just about make

 out seven Elders arriving, each in navy and greys. 'Five and seven, twelve so far,' Ellie thought to herself and hoped only a couple more were to arrive.

The winds began to pick up and Bryony, and Ellie, who still had her great grandmother's one, had to hold onto their hats to stop them from flying away.

Four more Weather Witches arrived, flying in on the winds from the West. Suddenly there was a bolt of lightning which lit up the skies. The air became warmer and the lightning was followed immediately by an almighty crash of thunder. Both girls crouched further down and hugged one another.

'The southern Weather Witches are arriving,' Bryony whispered to Ellie pointing to the sky, her voice shaking. Ellie was too scared to look as the four Elders flew in from the South. The weather though seemed to calm slightly. Bright, beautiful, colours swirled in the air; Ellie peered from her hiding place and saw Maeve and Elodie Mayweather arriving with Bryony's mother and four other elders.

Chapter 10

Let the Storms Come!

The elder Weather Witches each took their places around the meeting place with the Weather Rock behind them, and the Mayweather sisters in front.

Bryony and Ellie crouched down, hiding behind the large rock as the elders gathered in a circle. The atmosphere was heavy and they could hear thunder growling in the distance. Both girls shivered.

A witch stepped forward. She was tall with long, white hair and a stern look on her face. She raised her right hand and there was silence.

Ellie peeked over the rock and saw that her hat was light grey and had a snowflake on the point. She shuddered again and ducked back down.

'Sisters,' the witch began, 'we are here again and weaker still, yet no one has the answer. Are we all to disappear like our Earth sisters?'

'Let the storms come,' a voice called out. There was an eruption of gasps and shouts from the elders as they looked to see who had spoken. The voice continued louder and stronger. 'Let the storms come and let them wipe them out, only then can we rise up.'

It was Bryony now who peered over the rock. She saw a small woman with a hunchback and a walking stick. Her hair was slicked back in a bun and her hat was black with a thunderbolt at the tip. She stepped into the circle and the white Weather Witch stepped back.

'That's Audra, a southern Weather Witch, she's even grumpier than Elodie,' Bryony whispered to Ellie.

'You surely cannot believe or even want that?' a familiar voice entered the fray — it was Elodie.

'Why not?' replied Audra 'Have we not done all we can for the earth and atmosphere? Are our efforts all being counteracted by humans? If they were gone the elements would balance and the earth would be happy again, we would be happy again, our magic returned.'

There were many ripples of agreement in the circle. This terrified Ellie. Elodie too looked scared and almost lost for words.

Maeve stepped forward. 'But they can learn to look after the earth and we then can focus on the skies, then the elements can balance. How would we be happy having both earth *and* skies to look after?' Thankfully there seemed to be a few more murmurs of agreement following Maeve's point.

Audra became angered and stamped her walking stick down hard. A crackle of thunder sounded loudly over their heads. Hailstones beat down sharply around the witches as Winter, the white-haired Weather Witch, re-entered the circle with the other four elders from the North. The hailstones lasted only seconds but were enough to stop the thunder in its tracks.

'We stand with the Mayweathers — Maeve speaks sense — Humankind *can* learn.' Winter spoke calmly but firmly.

The three elders from the South gathered around Audra, followed by the seven elders from the East, making it clear where their allegiance lay.

'So, it is down to the elders from the West to decide our plan — waste our time trying to teach the humans or focus on our own survival and let the storms wipe the humans out?' Audra turned to the remaining group.

The westerly Weather Witches huddled together to talk through their decision. The winds picked up and swirled around them making a small tornado which engulfed the four huddled bodies.

Audra and the Mayweathers watched intently — both willing the westerly Witches to choose to stand with them. As the wind died down the head elder, Rosabel, stepped forward.

'Both make fair points. Maybe the Humans *could* learn to look after the Earth but we do not know if there is time enough to teach them or if they would be willing to listen. Time is against us all. We have little choice but to stand with the southern and eastern Weather Witches.' A cheer rose up from Audra and her followers.

Ellie and Bryony's hearts sank; Ellie whispered to Bryony 'That makes fifteen against twelve, they're sure to overpower them.'

Bryony shook her head and whispered back, 'The elders from this land have mastered *all* the weather systems so should be stronger than Audra and the others, especially now we have the northern witches standing with us.' Bryony tried to sound confident even though she wasn't actually sure their magic was strong enough.

'Elodie, Maeve, Winter — you see the majority vote is with me. Stand down — you cannot win this,' Audra stepped towards the Mayweathers, a sly, smug smile on her face.

'It is time for you to send the young Weather Witches to their final stations so they can become masters of their chosen weather elements and help in our fight. There's no reason, or point, for them to stay here any longer.'

'Yes,' Rosabel said stepping forward, 'we've heard some of the youngsters need more discipline in order to succeed, we'll be sure to get them up to scratch.' Her snide remark was aimed at Bryony's mother and did not go unnoticed. As soon as the last words had left her mouth a rain cloud appeared over her head and rained — hard — on her. Furious, Rosabel blew a gust of wind throwing Bryony's mother off her feet. As Bryony's mother stood up and dusted herself off, a mix of rain, wind and thunder began over their heads. Maeve raised her hands high and cast the storm clouds apart.

'Sisters,' she spoke clearly and loudly, 'this is not going to help anyone. I will *not* let you take the youngsters yet, there is still much for them to learn. I will also *not* allow you to let the storms come and destroy any more things than they have done already. We will help the humans.' With that she cast her bright, beautiful light at the elders standing against her, causing them to retreat a little.

Once the light had faded, Audra raised her stick high above her head. A large black storm cloud appeared. The elders next to her raised their weather stones and the storm cloud grew bigger and bigger. Wind, rain, thunder and lightning all enveloped in a thick black blanket covering the skies and blocking the way back to Ellie's land. 'Get past that!' She spat furiously.

Winter hurled hail stones across to Audra's side causing some of the Weather Witches to be knocked to the ground. The storm cloud shuddered but continued to grow. Maeve and Elodie's Witches created a hurricane and cast it upon Audra, making her stumble back. She looked furiously back at them, but before she could retaliate Ellie, filled with an anger of her own, stood up and shouted, loudly, 'STOP!'

Chapter 11

We Are Here! We Stand with You!

Ellie steadied herself against the Weather Rock she and Bryony had been hiding behind. As she did, the rock lit up with colour and the crack that had appeared earlier in the day shone a brilliant emerald green. A blinding light shot up from Ellie through the rock and up to the sky. There was silence.

Ellie was as shocked as everyone else. She looked down at her mother's necklace and saw that it too was glowing emerald green. She closed her eyes and felt she could hear whispers urging her on – could they be the past Earth Witches? 'We are here,' they seemed to say, 'we stand with you.'

Ellie opened her eyes and stared at the elders, trying not to let them hear the fear in her voice. She started to speak 'The Earth Witches are not dead, WE are still here, WE need to unite our magic to overcome the storms. Will you stand with me?'

Audra was bubbling with fury — she raised her stick above her head. Another black cloud appeared, and a lightning bolt shot down aimed straight at Ellie. Ellie cowered, terrified as to what was about to happen to her. She closed her eyes — waiting for the impact — but it never came.

Slowly she opened her eyes and could see a blue shimmering dome covering her. 'Run!' a voice bellowed. She looked around 'Run Ellie! Run now! We can't hold the lightning back for long!' It was the Mayweather sisters.

Bryony grabbed Ellie's hand and pulled her away. They ran as fast as they could.

'I always knew Audra was grumpy, but I never thought she was crazy to boot!' Bryony said breathlessly as they reached the cobbled streets.

'It didn't work!' Ellie shouted as they continued to run 'They didn't listen...'

'They may not have listened, but they saw!' Bryony interrupted 'Everyone in the land saw! The magic you created was beyond anything I could have imagined.'

Suddenly, from above they saw a blinding flash of lightning which lit up the skies followed by another almighty crack of thunder. They glanced back and could see nothing but a black cloud growing bigger and bigger.

'I'll have to get the others!' shouted Bryony as they ran down the streets. 'You hide, while I get back up. I'll be faster on my broom.' With that the girls separated. Bryony mounted her broom and zoomed off through the skies.

'Hazel!' Bryony hovered outside her sister's window. 'The plan — it's working! You have to come and help! We need *all* the Weather Witches to help! Come on, follow me!' Bryony didn't wait for a response; she had already gathered up a good number of young Weather Witches along the way and was too busy to stop.

Hazel hesitated, torn between her mother's orders and her sister's headstrong, crazy behaviour, then grabbing her weather stone, cloak and broom she flew off after her sister and the growing number of Weather Witches.

Back at the meeting the skies had erupted in storms of all kinds. In an attempt to overpower the other, both sides were causing more and more destructive winds and rain to be called up. Maeve and Elodie could feel the storms would soon be too great for any of the

Weather Witches' magic to control but Audra didn't seem to care.

'Make a distraction,' Elodie said to Maeve. Maeve summoned with all her strength the brightest, most dazzling Aurora Borealis display she could while Elodie snuck away to the streets.

Audra cackled, 'I used to always long to be able to call and create the Northern Lights then I realised electricity was far stronger!' A bolt of lightning lit up the sky, the Northern Lights vanished. Maeve, shocked by the strength of the bolt, knew she would have to fight lightning with lightning. She called upon bolt after bolt, but Audra knocked them away. Maeve could feel her magic weakening. Audra could see it too – choosing her time to strike when she felt Maeve was at her weakest. A bolt flew across the meeting place and struck Maeve. The electricity shot through to the other witches standing with her, jolting them all to the ground with a thud.

Audra and her followers walked up to the stunned bodies and, stepping over them, Audra said to Maeve with a sneer, 'Jack of all trades, master of none. Now to deal with that twin of yours and that brat of a child.'

Exhausted, Maeve could do nothing but watch them walk down to the houses, a tear rolled down her cheek.

Chapter 12

The Calling of the Emerald House

Ellie darted down the next alley she came to. Something seemed to be guiding her this way. Stopping to catch her breath momentarily, she looked up and saw, at the end of the alleyway, the emerald green house she had been drawn to the first day she arrived in this land.

Ellie ran towards the house; it felt as though it was willing her to come. She got to the door and pushed as hard as she could.

 The door was heavy, but Ellie managed to prise it open just enough for her to squeeze through. It shut with a thud behind her. Ellie leant back against the door trying to catch her breath. Looking

around she could see this wasn't a house that was lived in, it looked more like a laboratory. There was a lot of machinery and what looked like a radio phone.

Hung up on the wall was a huge map of the world. On it the land was mainly coloured black rather than the green Ellie would have expected. Next to the map was a list of names – many with a red cross through them and a couple with a circle around them followed by a question mark.

The rain thundered down outside and the winds blew wildly. Ellie walked slowly towards the list of names and tried to figure out what all this meant. As she looked back towards the map, she noticed it was changing. More of the green land was turning black and fast.

Another clash of thunder sounded outside, it seemed to be getting closer. Ellie shivered. She hoped Bryony was safe. She walked over to the radio phone and couldn't help but twiddle the buttons. The phone crackled and Ellie felt sure she had heard a voice. She put her head closer to the speaker and tried to make out what the voice was saying.

The door suddenly flung open and a figure stood tall in the doorway. A flash of lightning lit up the sky behind and Ellie saw that the figure was

Elodie. Ellie dropped to the ground and crawled under the desk she had been standing by.

Elodie ran in and slammed the door shut, she hadn't noticed Ellie hiding. She ran up to the radio phone and turned it on full and called frantically through the receiver, 'This is Elodie Mayweather, Weather Witch, we know you are out there, please, please respond. Earth Sisters we need you!' A crackle again came through the speaker, then a clear loud voice answered, 'We are here! We stand with you!' The radio phone spluttered and crackled some more and was then silent.

'Finally! I knew it!' Elodie cackled with delight and relief, throwing her arms in the air triumphantly.

The storms seemed to be surrounding the house now. Suddenly a great bolt of blinding white light crashed into the heavy oak door and split it in two. The wind and rain flew into the house followed by Audra and her followers. Ellie held her breath, frozen with fear, as she tried to make herself as small as she could.

Elodie raised her weather stone and her hat lit up with swirling colours, so bright they dazzled the elders. The wind and rain calmed a little.

'Listen,' Elodie shouted above the noise, 'I have proof the Earth Witches are still here and how to find them!' She reached for the radio phone. A high-pitched scream filled the room making Elodie and the other witches freeze. Audra raised her stick and cast a bolt of lightning, smashing the phone to pieces.

'Lies!' She hissed 'The Earth Witches are all dead! I helped see to that!'

Despite the raging storms, the room became silent. The elder Weather Witches who had followed Audra stood mouths agape at these final words that clearly showed what her real motives had been. They had been fooled.

Outside, the storm clouds continued to grow. They were now far too strong for the Weather Witches to control and the realisation of what they had done started to sink in.

'Elodie, we're so sorry,' Rosabel cried 'what can we do to stop this?' Elodie did not have the answers.

'Weak!' Audra shouted 'You're all weak! We don't need to do anything but watch — watch the storms destroy the humans.'

'They will destroy our land too,' Elodie said. 'The only way we can save our worlds is to do what Ellie said — combine our magic with the Earth Witches but with the radio phone destroyed I don't know how we are going to get to them now.'

Ellie bravely crawled out from her hiding place, 'I'm here and I'm an Earth Witch descendant, could I help?' she said, her voice small and wavering. All eyes looked to Ellie but before anyone could answer Audra darted across the room on her broom and seized her. Holding Ellie tightly she flew out of the house and up into the stormy skies.

'No!' Elodie screamed reaching up to no avail as Audra flew higher and higher into the storm clouds overhead, Ellie in her grasp too terrified to fight against her. Elodie grabbed her broom and shot up after Audra and Ellie.

Chapter 13

Magic Combined

The winds were blowing strong but the young Weather Witches held tight to their brooms and forced their way through. Hazel was darting and diving trying to make her way to Bryony.

'My door is still shut tight!' Hazel shouted at Bryony 'I had to climb out of the window! Where's Ellie?'

'Down there,' Bryony said pointing down to the emerald house.

'At the old weather station?' Hazel quizzed. 'How do you know?' Bryony pointed again – this time at the storms that were swirling all around it. 'I'm going in to get her and then we're going save our worlds,' she shouted with confidence.

Hazel looked behind them and saw, what seemed to be hundreds of young

Weather Witches all holding their own through the blinding wind and rain.

'Guide them through to Ellie's land and we'll meet you there! Trust me!' Bryony called to Hazel and started to fly down towards the emerald house. Hazel nodded. 'Follow me!' she called to the Weather Witches and flew harder towards Ellie's land.

The clouds were thick and the power in them was far stronger than Hazel had ever seen. The young Weather Witches were being blown this way and that trying to find a break in the cloud to get through.

Almost giving up, Hazel remembered a spell from the forbidden book, 'Spells and Magic for the Curious Witch', and, having nothing else to lose, she held her weather stone high and shouted with all her might 'Scamaill stoirme! Speartha oscailte!' A bolt of light flew from her stone into the clouds and a crack appeared; it was small but Hazel thought it was just enough for the young Weather Witches to fit through.

'Quickly!' She called back to the others, unsure of how long the spell would last, 'fly through the break in the clouds as fast as you can!' The Weather Witches may have been young but they flew strongly and bravely, one after another, into Ellie's land.

Ellie's mother was standing by the oak tree looking up to the stormy skies. She knew something dreadful was happening — she feared for Ellie and her heart was racing. Suddenly she saw a small split in the cloud. As she stared into the sky she saw a young Weather Witch slip through the gap. The one quickly became many and as each Weather Witch landed she told them, 'Head into the house, you'll be safe there.'

Ellie's mother stayed outside until the last witch flew down. It was Hazel, and just as she flew through the cloud the opening closed tight behind her and the cloud grew even bigger. Ellie's mother's heart sank 'Where's Ellie?' she asked Hazel in a panic. Hazel looked down. 'Right,' Ellie's mother said, 'into the house dry yourself off and tell me everything you know.' Hazel hurried in to join the others.

The young Weather Witches all gathered in the kitchen and Hazel filled everyone in about the events from the day.

Hazel hardly knew where to start. The young Weather Witches had all gathered in the kitchen in a noisy and confused rabble. They had been waiting for something to

happen ever since the elders had first gathered to talk about the changing weather systems — the elders seemed so divided in their views on what needed to be done.

The day after the meeting Bryony had called all the young witches together. If the elders were divided, she had said, the young witches must stand together. They had all cheered in agreement and had been eagerly awaiting their time. When Bryony and Hazel had summoned them in the midst of the storms they had followed without question because they trusted their friends but it was not until now that they really grasped how serious an adventure this was.

'Ok, listen up!' shouted Hazel. Slowly the chattering ceased and Hazel continued. She looked mainly towards Ellie's mum as she related the events of the past few days. 'The elders can't seem to agree what to do. Now they are arguing and calling up more storms,' she continued, 'but if the storms grow much bigger even the elders' magic will not be strong enough to control them.' Hazel saw all the worried faces around her, 'But Ellie, Bryony's friend — had an idea — if we combine our magic

 with the Earth Witches' magic, together we would be powerful enough to balance the elements, stop the storms getting out of control and start to mend the Earth.' 'But the Earth Witches are all gone,' the young witches murmured.

Ellie's mother stepped forward 'Not all of us,' she said. 'follow me,' and with that she ran back out into the garden through the wind and the rain to the old oak tree — the young witches following closely behind.

Ellie's Mum placed her forehead on the trunk of the oak tree as if she was greeting someone. She placed her left palm flat against the trunk and began whispering very quietly.

'Why is she talking to a tree?' one of the Weather Witches asked, puzzled. 'It's not just a tree — that's her grandmother,' Hazel began to explain then, deciding another time would be best, ended by saying, 'it's a long story just follow her lead — trust me.'

'Hazel, get everyone to gather round so they can touch the tree,' said Ellie's Mum. Hazel did so. Some of the witches had to fly up on their brooms to be able to reach the tree. Once each witch's left palm was placed flat against the oak tree's trunk, their weather stones began to glow and the trunk began to pulse with light. The ground shook.

'Keep your contact!' shouted Ellie's mother as she pressed harder against the tree. The light from the tree and all the weather stones became brighter and brighter, every colour you could imagine, the roots from

the tree shone through the soil that covered them. The colours shot high into the sky piercing the thick black cloud.

Chapter 14

A Storm Too Far

Bryony flew down towards the old weather station and as she did she saw Audra flying up into the sky. Bryony circled round trying to get a clearer view of what she was doing and saw, to her horror, that Audra had a tight grip on Ellie. Her heart sank.

Ellie was still frozen with fear. She could see thunder clouds all around her and then, from the corner of her eye she saw Audra's weather stone glowing a bright yellow. It was connected to the very top of Audra's walking stick which had been slid through her belt to secure it on the broom with her. Ellie started to think of a plan.

Elodie grabbed her broomstick and followed Audra and Ellie up into the stormy skies. As she flew after them she saw Bryony.

'Bryony,' she called as she flew to her, 'do *not* attempt to follow them — it is too dangerous, stay here, stay low and try not to be seen.' Bryony wanted so much to ignore these instructions, but she heard a fear in Elodie's voice she'd never heard before and knew this could be life or death. She watched as Elodie flew higher and higher. Elodie stopped and hovered just outside the thunder cloud that Audra had entered so confidently.

'Audra!' Elodie shouted. Nothing. 'Audra!' she called again, edging closer to the growing black cloud. Audra bolted out of the cloud shrieking, nearly knocking Elodie off her broom. She darted back into the cloud disappearing from sight.

'Are you scared Elodie?' Audra's voice taunted from deep within the cloud.

'Are you?' Elodie responded sharply 'Why else would you hide from me?'

Audra reappeared cackling 'Me? Scared of you? Don't make me laugh!' The storm cloud behind her rumbled and sparked with electricity pulses. 'I called this,' Audra said 'I control this.' As she crowed she loosened her grip on Ellie. Ellie took this chance to break a hand free and seized

Audra's walking stick, throwing it as hard as she could into the cloud behind.

Audra shrieked, dropping Ellie as she desperately reached out for the stick. Ellie fell quickly past Elodie's outstretched arms, tumbling through the sky. Audra grabbed her walking stick but as she did so a lightning bolt struck the weather stone at the top. Electricity shot down the stick and into Audra. She wailed and shrieked as the current sparked through her with such burning intensity, yet still she would not let go of her stick.

Ellie, still tumbling through the air heard the wail and the shriek, then suddenly felt a hand grab hers and pull her onto a broom hugging her tightly. It was Bryony! Elodie, Bryony and Ellie watched as, within seconds Audra exploded into the sky like a firework and nothing remained of her but dust.

The girls hugged each other tightly and Bryony flew them to the ground. 'You're safe!' They were so happy to see each other they almost forgot about the growing storms around them. Suddenly the ground shook.

Elodie flew down to join them, 'Quickly you two, get back to the Weather Rock.'

Bryony and Ellie ran back to the Weather Rock just as the elders were arriving on their brooms. 'Look!' shouted Ellie pointing upwards. A brilliant bright light had burst through the thick black cloud above cascading a shower of colour over the assembly of witches.

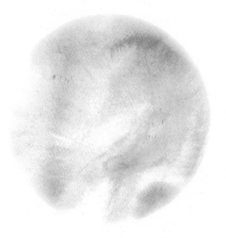

Chapter 15

Sealed with an Emerald Stone

By the time Ellie, Bryony and Elodie arrived at the Weather Rock, Maeve and the other elders who Audra had stunned were back on their feet, dishevelled but not too harmed. They were all gathered around the Weather Rock that was still shining with beautiful colours, the crack sealed with an emerald stone.

'You healed the rock,' Maeve said smiling at Ellie and opening her arms wide to embrace both girls, 'you brave, wonderful girls!' Bryony's mother too had run up to them both and hugged Bryony tightly. 'You scared me,' she said to Bryony, 'but my, am I proud!'

Ellie slowly walked up to the Weather Rock, 'But how?' she muttered as she studied the emerald.

'You must have the power of the Earth Witch, Heather — my great friend,' Elodie said smiling 'You certainly have her spirit! Your descendant... could it be...? Of course! I can't believe I hadn't seen it before.'

Bryony turned to her mother, 'The young Weather Witches are all in Ellie's land, with Hazel. Look' she said pointing to the light in the sky.

'You and your sister working together! Well! I never thought I'd see the day!' Her mother jested.

Elodie, cutting the moment short, addressed the group 'Elders, and you — Bryony, Ellie, we must all place our left palms flat on the Weather Rock.'

With that the group all huddled around the rock and placed their palms flat on it. As they did their weather stones and Ellie's necklace began to shine brightly. A pulse of light flew

from the Weather Rock up into the stormy skies and clashed against the light breaking through from Ellie's land causing sparks to fly.

The light merged and spread across the sky for a split second and then vanished.

'What's happening?' Ellie whispered to Bryony. Bryony just shrugged her shoulders.

'Look,' Winter said, pointing up to the skies with a huge smile on her face. Slowly the big black cloud began to break apart as if retreating and the stars could be seen again shining brightly.

'It's working!' Bryony said excitedly, 'your plan has worked!'

'For now,' Maeve said 'We've managed to control the storms for now. But the Earth still has a lot of healing to do. We, the Weather Witches, Earth Witches and the humans, must all work together and in time we may be able to heal it completely, hopefully.' Maeve looked hard at Elodie as she spoke.

In Ellie's land, the young Weather Witches watched as the bright light flashed across the skies and forced the storms to retreat. They slowly took their hands off the Oak tree, exhausted, but proud.

'We did it!' Hazel shouted in triumph raising her fist high. 'We did it!' the Weather Witches all chanted together.

Ellie's mother smiled as she watched the storm clouds soften but could not celebrate until she knew Ellie was safe.

'It is time for you to return to your land,' Ellie's mother said addressing the group. 'Well done, you did our lands proud.' Though exhausted, the Weather Witches were eager to get back home. After thanking her and bidding Ellie's mum farewell, one by one they flew up and disappeared to the land behind the clouds.

As Hazel went to leave, Ellie's mum turned to her, 'Hazel, please get Ellie home to me safely.'

'I will,' Hazel replied and off she flew up to the calm night skies.

Chapter 16

Farewell for Now

'Hazel and the others should be returning soon now that the skies are calm,' Bryony said to her mother.

'And we too should bid you farewell,' the elders said, each noticeably more humble than when they first arrived. Only a few snowflakes fell as Winter and the other northern Weather Witches left, no wild winds surrounded the westerly Weather Witches — just gentle breezes and only a light shower followed the easterly Weather Witches as they departed.

The southern Weather Witches, now with one less and still shocked by the treachery of their leader, left with no ill will. They apologised for Audra's behaviour and thanked Ellie for showing them the Earth Witches were still present. The witches all seemed more united, and calm, like the night skies above.

Dawn was fast approaching and Ellie was keen to get home to her land and her mother. Elodie and Maeve could see this in Ellie's face. 'Come on,' they said in unison, 'let's get back to the old weather station — that is where the safest pass-through point is to your land.'

With that they started to walk briskly towards the cobbled streets and the beautiful coloured houses. Ellie walked in between the Mayweathers and Bryony walked alongside, with her mother. Elodie was much chattier now and even had a smile, though slight, on her face.

'You see,' Elodie explained to Ellie as they approached the old weather station, 'Heather, your great grandmother, never said goodbye — so I thought the rumours were true. I tried for many, many years to find her, to find any of the Earth Witches, but to no avail. Some even said I grew a little bitter as the years passed as hope faded.'

Maeve, leaned across Ellie, 'Some? A little?' she quipped to Elodie. 'I believe everyone felt you became bitter and grumpy — very grumpy.' Ellie and Bryony giggled.

As they got closer they saw the young Weather Witches arriving back, each one descending slowly through the calm skies using the light from their weather stones to guide them through the dusky sky.

Hazel landed and ran over to Bryony looking like she was about to hug her then stopped. 'Glad to see you're ok,' she said bluntly, 'you still have to clean my door when we get home.' Their mother glanced at Bryony, eyebrows raised. Bryony rolled her eyes as she replied curtly to Hazel, 'And *you're* welcome for the amazing plan *Ellie and I* executed.'

'I helped!' argued Hazel, indignantly. This time it was their Mother who rolled her eyes. 'Girls, stop!' she said sternly. 'You have both done a fantastic job, I don't even want to *know* what Bryony has done to your door Hazel, but please stop now. Bryony, would you like to take Ellie back? But please come straight back home after.' Hazel grumbled and walked off as Bryony started to get her broom ready.

'Before you take Ellie back, I'd like to show her something,' Elodie said and led Ellie into the old weather station, stepping through the large crack in the heavy oak door. She walked straight up to the list of names Ellie had noticed on the wall when she had first entered the emerald-roofed building. 'These,' Elodie explained whilst removing the list from the wall, 'are potential Earth Witches that may still be able to practise, or are indeed still practising. I would get small snippets every now and then, but with the storms there was always doubt as to what actually was coming through the radio phone. Now it's smashed, I think you may have more luck finding any surviving

Earth Witches in your land. Would you do that for me?' Elodie asked hopefully.

'Of course!' Ellie said excitedly taking the list from Elodie, folding it neatly and placing it safely in her pocket (making sure it wasn't the holey one).

'Thank you,' Elodie said and turned to look at the map on the wall. Ellie stood there for a while and then, realising that this was Elodie's way of saying goodbye, she felt her cheeks blush a little and quickly walked out of the door, remembering to leave the photograph of her great grandmother and Elodie on the desk before she left.

'Are you ready?' Bryony asked Ellie as she emerged from the weather station.

'Hang on!' Hazel suddenly appeared, running down the street. 'If you're serious about becoming a practising Earth Witch you must read this,' she said to Ellie, passing her a very old and grubby book. Ellie looked at the red worn, tattered cover

— 'The Legend of Dragonfoot', it read. Slightly confused, Ellie smiled, thanked Hazel and holding the book tightly to her chest she climbed on the back of Bryony's broom.

'Goodbye everyone,' she said with a wave.

'We'll no doubt see you again, little Earth sister,' Maeve said with a broad grin and a big wave and with that Bryony flew up into the skies and through to Ellie's land.

Chapter 17

A Gift

The skies were quiet when Ellie arrived back and the sun was slowly rising. The friends said their goodbyes knowing they would see each other again soon and hopefully in less dire circumstances.

Ellie's mother hugged her tightly as they curled up on the sofa and spoke about the adventures she'd had. Her mother smiled as she listened and saw the magic in Ellie's eyes as she told

her story. They spoke until their eyes were too heavy to stay open and then they slept, exhausted, relieved and happy.

As the next day began, Ellie was keen to get out into the garden. She wanted to check the trees and plants were thriving. As she reached the oak tree Ellie noticed there was something leaning against it and as she got closer she could see it was a broom. Glancing around, Ellie expected to see Bryony but saw no one else – just the broom. Ellie looked closer at it and saw there was a small engraving on the side which read 'Ellie'. As she picked it up, slowly and carefully as though she feared it would break, a small note fell to the ground. Ellie picked it up. 'Dear Ellie, here is a thank you gift from us, Elodie and Maeve Mayweather'.

Ellie smiled and looked up to the sky just as a flash of colourful lights sparkled for a second then vanished.

The rain began to fall but Ellie continued to smile – she no longer minded a little bit of rain.

Glossary

'Solas na gréine' — Irish for 'Sunshine/Light of the sun'

'Scamaill agus gaoth' — Irish for 'Cloud and Wind'

'Scamaill stoirme! Speartha oscailte!' — Irish for 'Storm clouds! Open!'

Nimbostratus — Dark, grey clouds that produce rain

Aurora Borealis/Northern Lights — Characterised by streams of reddish and greenish lights in the sky caused by a natural electrical phenomenon

Weather stone — Based on the witches' stone/hag stone. Stones with a natural hole through them that are said to be magical; warding off evil and, some even say, by looking through the hole you can see into the magical world of fairy folk.

Seeds for thought...

Over the last 150 years humans have put lots of carbon dioxide into the sky which is hurting the Earth. One of the simplest and best things we can do is plant long-life hardwood trees that are native to the different areas in which we live. As Ellie's mother told her, trees absorb carbon dioxide and release oxygen, helping to balance the elements. Here are a few examples of the best trees for doing this:

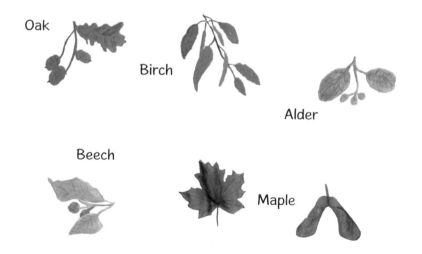

Oak

Birch

Alder

Beech

Maple